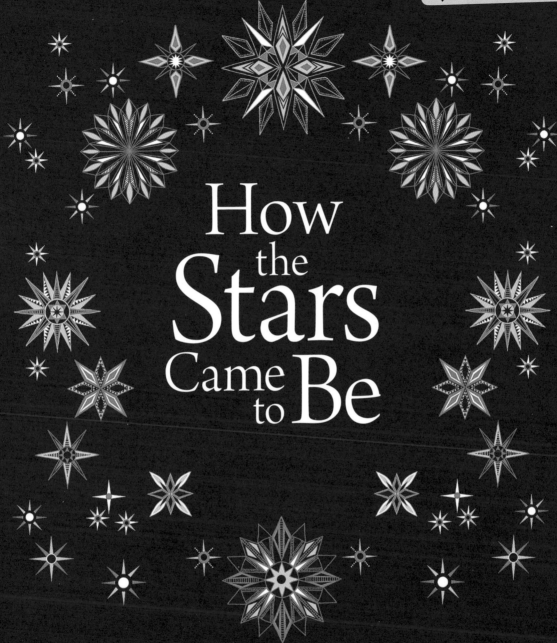

How the Stars Came to Be

Poonam Mistry

In a time many years ago, there was only the light from the Sun and the Moon.

There once lived a Fisherman's daughter who loved to feel the light on her skin. During the day, she would dance and play, weaving in and out of the Sun's rays.

And at night she would push back the curtains, lie in the cool glow and think
of her father working at sea, guided only by the light of the Moon.

However, for a few nights each
month the Moon would completely disappear,
slipping from sight and leaving the Fisherman
out at sea alone in the darkness.

The Girl worried about her father and how he would find his way home safely.

One morning as the Sun spread
light over the land, the Girl could
be found crying in the corner of her room.

"My dear, whatever is the matter?" the Sun asked,
gently warming the light that surrounded her.

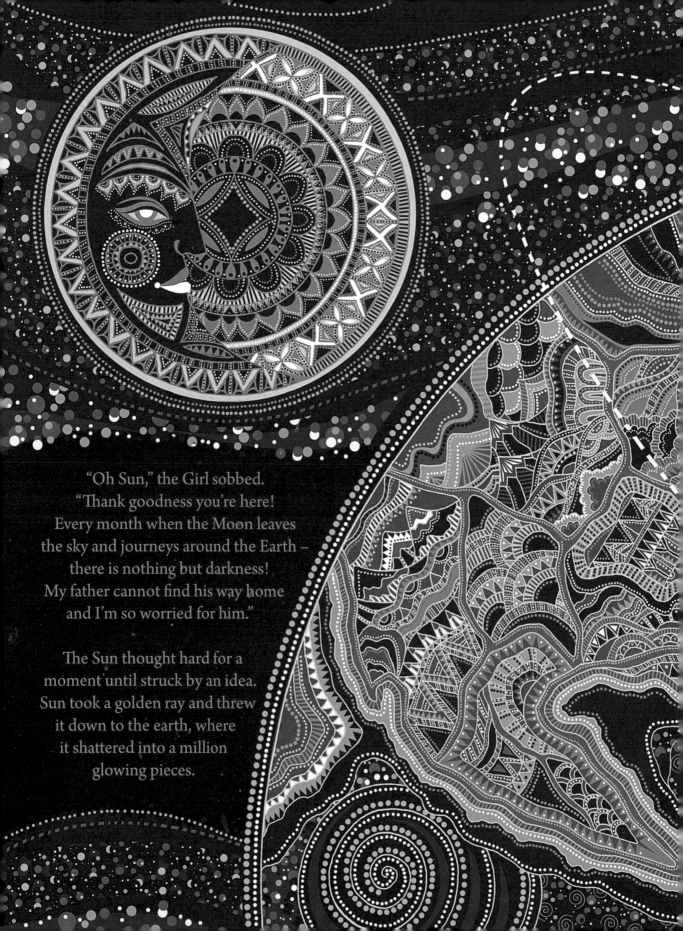

"Oh Sun," the Girl sobbed.
"Thank goodness you're here!
Every month when the Moon leaves
the sky and journeys around the Earth –
there is nothing but darkness!
My father cannot find his way home
and I'm so worried for him."

The Sun thought hard for a
moment until struck by an idea.
Sun took a golden ray and threw
it down to the earth, where
it shattered into a million
glowing pieces.

"Gather together all the shining pieces I've given you. Then tonight when I drop beneath the horizon and the light dims, place each of them into the sky. They will glisten and shine, providing you with my light on the deepest and darkest nights. We will call them stars."

That night, the Fisherman's daughter
climbed to the top of the highest mountain
and, at the point where the sky meets the
Earth, she began carefully placing each
of the Sun's stars into the deep
navy fabric of the sky.

She started with the brightest star. Reaching
up, she placed it directly above her head.

"You will be called Polaris," she announced.
"And you will point the way North!"

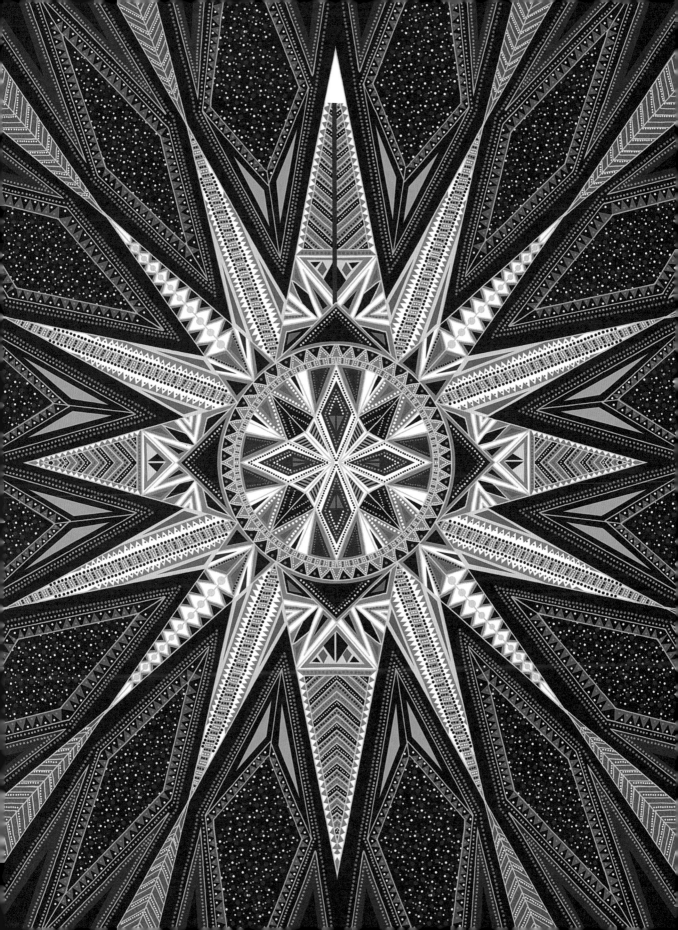

She slowly and carefully began to
arrange the stars into the sky, creating
beautiful pictures and images.

Soon the word spread and the Girl's
pictures were known across the land.

Animals came from far and wide
to have their portraits pinned
into the sky.

She worked tirelessly each evening, week after week,
paying special attention to the placement
of each and every tiny star.

But after a few months, she looked down into her bag and
her smile fell. Despite all her hard work, there were still so many
stars left – this would take her longer than forever.
The task was impossible!

But while the
Girl had been
putting the
stars
into the sky,
a Monkey had been
watching her carefully.
Sitting on the branch of his
favourite tree,
the glistening stars had
caught his eye!
As the Girl sat with her head
in her hands, the Monkey
slowly crept down the tree
and headed towards
the bag.

He just wanted to touch one! Surely one touch wouldn't hurt? But he couldn't resist and quickly snatched the whole bag and raced back towards the tree. "Wait, stop!" the Girl cried, as she watched the Monkey's tail shoot up the trunk and disappear into the depths of the branches.

The Girl started to climb after him.
Higher and higher, the monkey went,
so higher and higher she climbed after him
until they reached the very top of the tree.
"Give me the bag!" she cried, reaching out
to catch hold of the strap.

The Monkey and the Girl fought over
the bag, pulling it back and forth.

Suddenly, the Monkey let go!

"Oh no!" the Girl cried. "Look what you made me do! You've ruined my beautiful pictures."

The stars flew out of the bag and up into the night sky, creating a huge smudge across the Fisherman's daughter's work.

But just then, something caught the Girl's eye. As she looked out to the sea, she could see something illuminated by this new streak of glistening stars . . . it was her father's boat.

When she looked around, the smudge of stars had lit up the entire landscape as far as the eye could see.

Everyone came out of their homes to see the beautiful sparkles that lit up the night sky, and they marvelled at the astonishing new arc of stars that the Monkey had accidentally created.

From then on, the Fisherman was able to find his way home safely every night.
And this is how the stars came to be.

For my twin sister Priya
and all the other junior doctors and NHS workers.

You are all stars.

First published 2019 by order of the Tate Trustees
by Tate Publishing, a division of Tate Enterprises Ltd,
Millbank, London SW1P 4RG

www.tate.org.uk/publishing

Text and artwork © Poonam Mistry
First published 2019

ISBN 978 1 84976 663 0

Distributed in the United States and Canada by ABRAMS, New York
Library of Congress Control Number applied for
Printed and bound in China by C&C Offset Printing Co., Ltd
Colour Reproduction by DL Imaging, London